The Art Teacher
from the
Black Lagoon

by Mike Thaler · pictures by Jared Lee

SCHOLASTIC INC.

New York   Toronto   London   Auckland   Sydney
Mexico City   New Delhi   Hong Kong   Buenos Aires

visit us at www.abdopublishing.com

Reinforced library bound edition published in 2012 by Spotlight,
a division of the ABDO Group, PO Box 398166, Minneapolis, MN 55439. Spotlight produces high-quality
reinforced library bound editions for schools and libraries. Published by agreement with Scholastic Inc.

Printed in the United States of America, North Mankato, Minnesota.
102011
012012
This book contains at least 10% recycled materials.

For Erica and all The Glitter Queens
—M.T.

To good ol'
JOHN HERRON ART INSTITUTE
—J.L.

Cataloging-in-Publication Data

Thaler, Mike, 1936-
  The art teacher from the Black Lagoon / by Mike Thaler ; pictures by Jared Lee.
    p. cm.
[1. Art teachers—Juvenile fiction. 2. Art—Juvenile fiction. 3. Elementary schools—Juvenile fiction.]
PZ7.T3 Sd 2003
[E}-dc22
ISBN 978-1-59961-952-1 (reinforced library edition)

All Spotlight books are reinforced library bindings
and manufactured in the United States of America.

Today, I have my first art class.

The teacher's name is Krayolla Swamp. The kids call her the "Glitter Queen" because she leaves a trail of sparkles wherever she goes.

They say sometimes she makes her dresses out of egg cartons, her jewelry out of pipe cleaners, and her hats out of paper plates.

She wears a long ponytail that she paints with, and she has a big *weasel* that she paints on.

Her room is supposed to be a recycling dump.

And her closets—forget it! They're still looking for a kid who opened one.

They say she tells you to *express* yourself. I want to draw dinosaurs biting each other's heads off. But she makes you draw flowers, clouds, and other girl stuff.

And they say you have to paint with your fingers. Gross! I'm wearing gloves.

And then she makes you paint with your feet. Some kids will never have to wear socks again.

You can really *slop* around because there's *pig-ment* and *Sty-rofoam* everywhere.

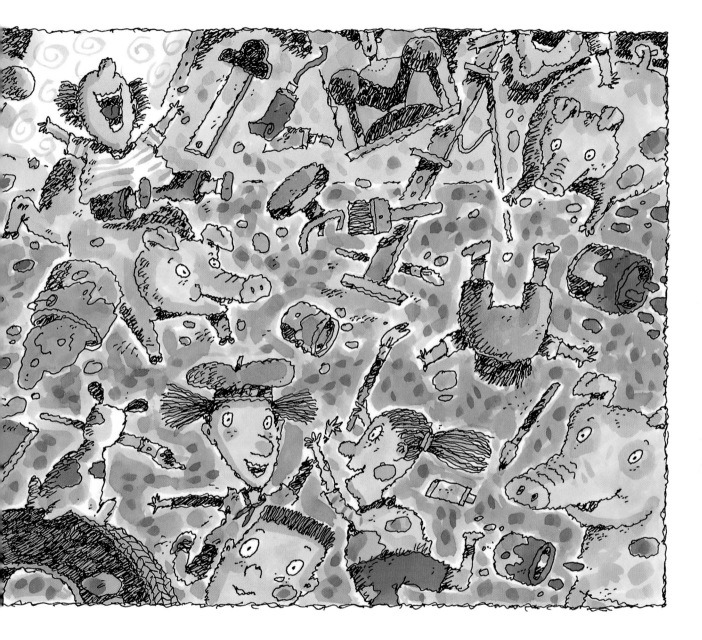

Some kids throw paint and have *tempera* tantrums.

On Valentine's Day, you have to cut out hearts. That could get messy.

Then there's the clay that's *really* messy and
squishy! She puts you on a wheel and spins you
around until you're frizzy and dizzy.

Then she sticks you in an oven and fires you! Can I get *fired* from school?

They say that you come out of her class with a real *glazed* look.

Then there's *mobiles*. Some kids are still
hanging around her room.

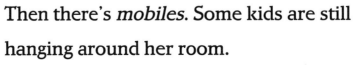

A kid named "Art" and a kid named "Matt" got framed and hung on the wall.

They say she has pots full of glue, and some kids end up sticking to their projects for a long time.

I heard you learn how to fold cookies into different shapes. It's called *oreo-gami*.

And then you have to learn about *artists*. There was a whole bunch of them, and they were *all* a little weird.

One artist lay on his back for four years and painted a ceiling. He should have used a roller. It would have been much quicker!

And there's another guy who cut off his ear and mailed it to *Erie*, Pennsylvania!

Their paintings are weird, too. This one guy named "Dolly"
painted wacky watches.

 And a guy named P. Catso painted melted Martians!

But most of them just painted their own thumbs.

My dad says people become artists because they can't get regular jobs.

Well, it's time to go to art class. We march in.

Wow! There's a big rainbow on the wall. It's awesome!

Miss Swamp says we can use every color in it. I'm gonna paint rainbow dinosaurs biting each other's heads off.

I'm gonna love art. Maybe I'll even be an artist someday.